The Seed Surprise

by Julie Verne
illustrated by Bill Ogden

Harcourt

Orlando   Boston   Dallas   Chicago   San Diego

Visit *The Learning Site!*

www.harcourtschool.com

Sam sees something growing outside in his yard. "What will this little sprout grow into?" he wonders.

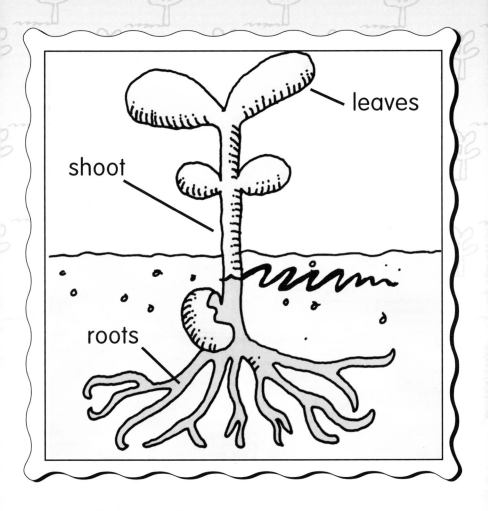

Sam thinks about the little plant growing in the soil. He wonders what it will look like.

Sam's dog, Rex, likes to dig. Sam
protects the little plant. He puts a little
fence around it.

The plant needs sunlight and water
to grow. When no rain falls, Sam
waters it.

By summer, the plant is growing very
fast. Its stems grow long. Sam thinks
it looks bigger every day.

One day, Sam sees beautiful yellow flowers on the plant. "Stay away, Rex," says Sam. "These flowers are not for you."

Sam is surprised when the yellow flowers turn into small, green pumpkins. Now Sam knows what kind of plant it is.

The pumpkins grow and turn orange.
As each one ripens, Sam's dad cuts
it off the plant. Sam scoops out
the seeds.

Sam washes the smooth pumpkins in one of the streams near his house. He gives two to his mom. Pumpkins are full of nutrition and good to eat.

Sam cuts faces into the rest of his pumpkins. He notices the pumpkin seeds on the ground. He sees his dog digging in the soil. Sam thinks he knows what will happen.

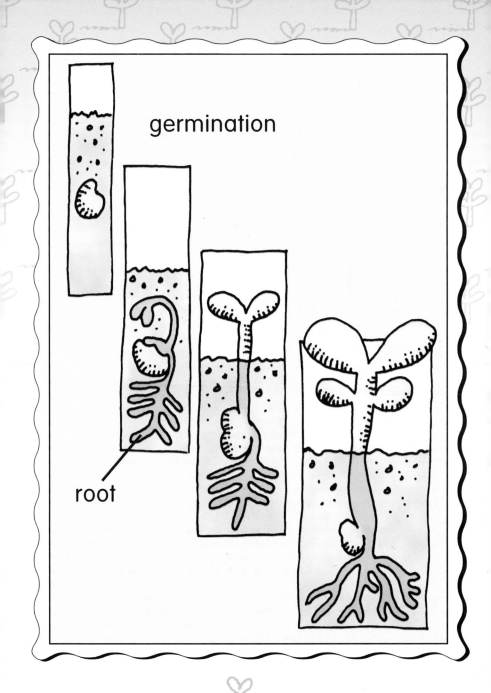

germination

root

The next spring, Sam sees a lot of green sprouts in his yard. They look like the pumpkin plant he grew last year. Sam protects and waters the plants.

14

When all of the pumpkins ripen, Sam
has too many! He calls his friends.
They are happy to get Sam's
pumpkins.

Some of Sam's friends help him. They
know just what to do. So does Rex!
He knows it's time to dig in the soil
and plant more pumpkin seeds!